D0819493

For Joel,
Charlie and Seth
~ J.C.

tiger tales
5 River Road, Suite 128, Wilton, CT 06897
Published in the United States 2015
Originally published in Great Britain 2015
by Little Tiger Press
Text and illustrations copyright © 2015 Jane Chapman
Visit Jane Chapman at www.ChapmanandWarnes.com
ISBN-13: 978-1-58925-195-3
ISBN-10: 1-58925-195-4
Printed in China
LTP/1400/1134/0315

For more insight and activities, visit us at
www.tigertalesbooks.com

JANE CHAPMAN

NO MORE CUDDLES!

tiger tales

Barry lived by himself deep in the forest.
He liked strolling around on his own, listening
to the birds, and eating juicy berries.
But Barry was **never** on his own for long . . . .

...Barry was **smothered** in **cuddles.**

Barry liked cuddling, **of course he did.**
But he was fed up with being smoothed
and stroked, and patted and fluffed

all the time.

"I just want to be **alone**," he sighed.
"I know. I'll make a disguise,
so no one will know it's me!"

But Barry's disguise **didn't work** at all.

"Maybe if I was a little more scary?"

he wondered.

So he put on an **angry** face and growled,

"GRRRRRRRRRR!"

"Oh, poor Cuddle Monster!" said Badger.
"Are you a bit **grumpy** today?"

"Hey, everyone! Barry needs a snuggle-buggle!"

Barry groaned. The cuddles had to STOP!

So he painted a **huge** sign.

Lots of animals wanted the job.
But none of them was
quite right.

"Too tiny!"

"Too spiky!"

"Too
stinky!"

Barry was about to give up
when he saw . . .

Bear was **perfect!**
His tummy was snuggly.
His fur was silky.
And his hug was
just right.

Barry was delighted.

"Bunnies, badger, beaver!"

he called.

"Anyone want a cuddle?"

"Me!"

"Me! Me!
I want a cuddle!"
the animals cried.
Big and small, they
rushed as fast as they
could toward Bear . . .

...and **zoomed** straight past him!
"What are you doing?" cried Barry.
"Don't cuddle me—

cuddle Bear!"

But it was too late.
The animals threw
themselves at Barry.

Barry wibbled.
He wobbled. Then he
toppled right over . . .

SPLAT!

...right into the **swamp**.
The swamp was
slimy, mucky,
and yucky.

The animals looked at Barry in horror.
"Where has all the fluffy gone?"
they cried.
"He's not snuggly at all!"
One by one the animals
hopped off to get clean . . .

. . . leaving Barry all by himself.

"No more cuddles for me,"

he grinned. "Well, not for a little while, anyway!"
Then he wiggled his huge toes, smiled
his **enormous** smile, and settled
down happily into the mud.
Peace at last!